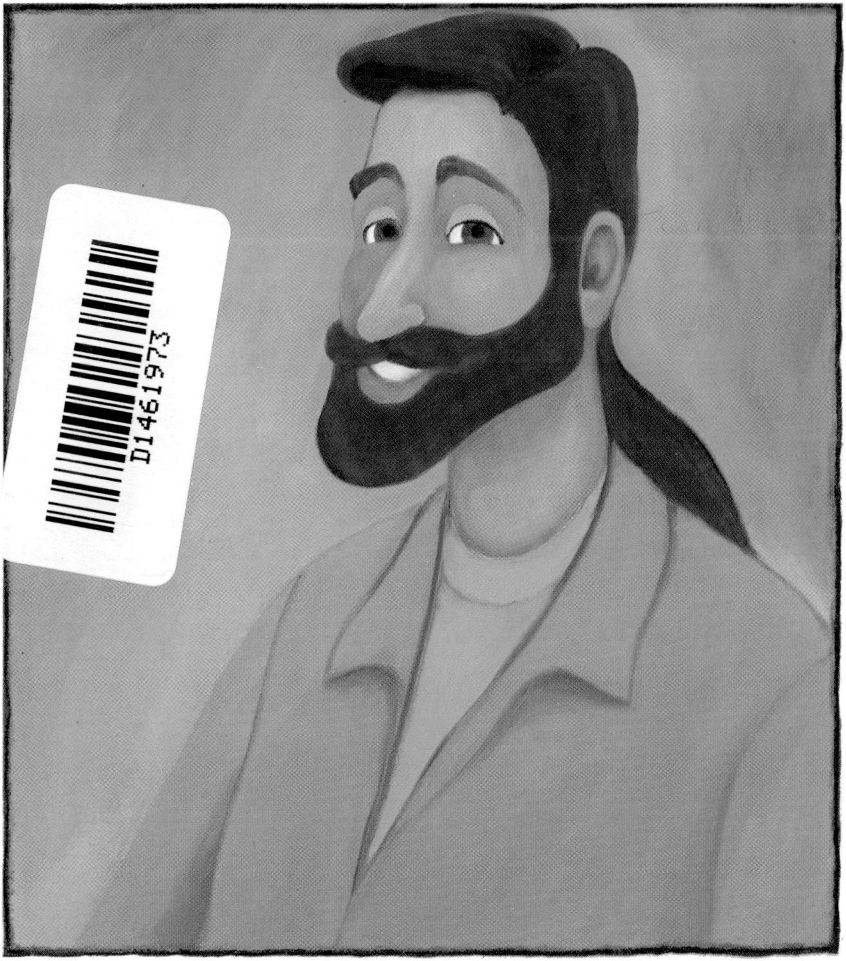

The Toy Maker

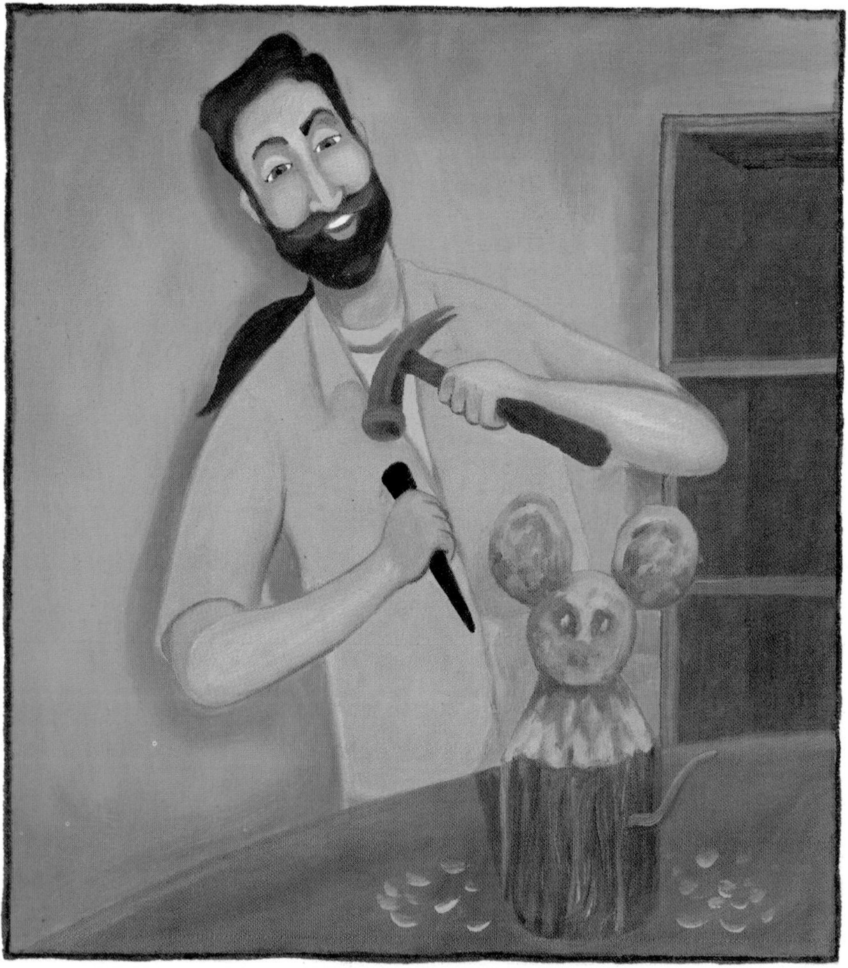

The man made a mouse.

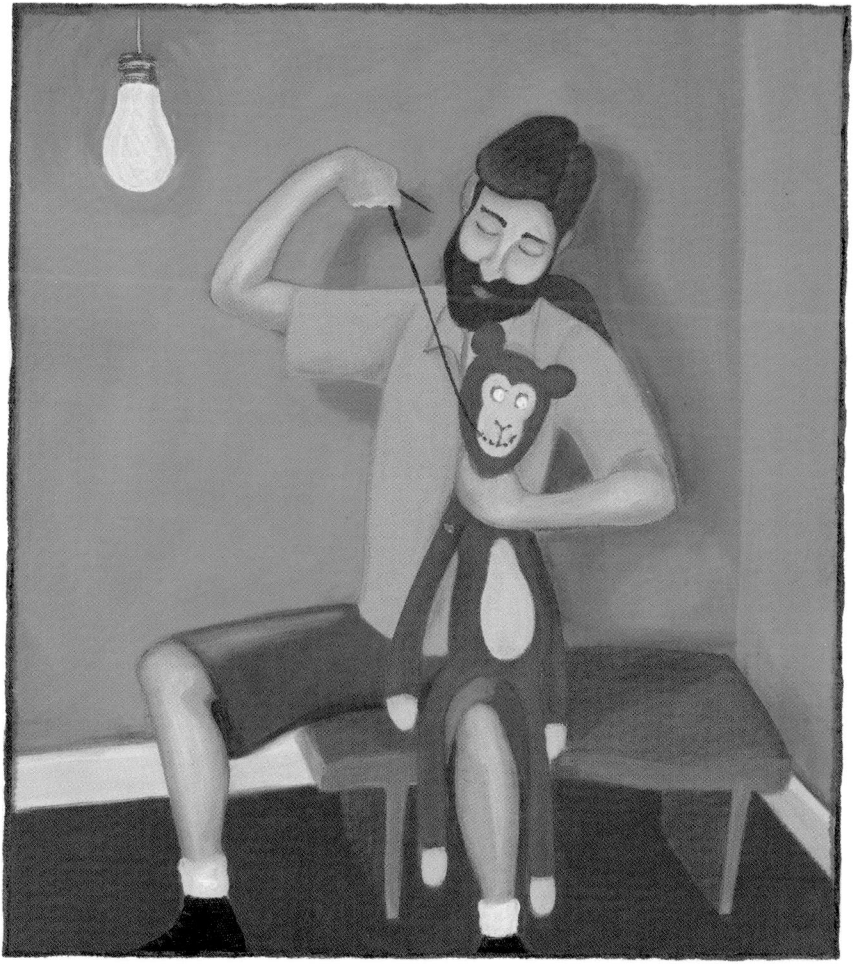

The man made a monkey.

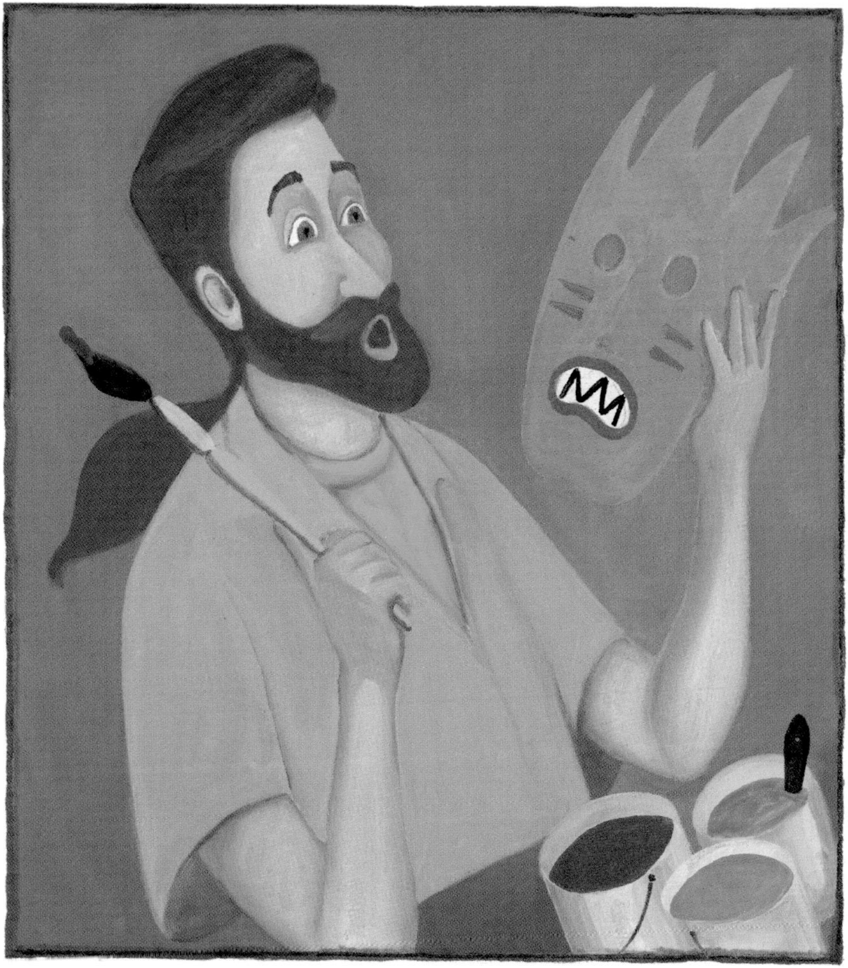

The man made a mask.

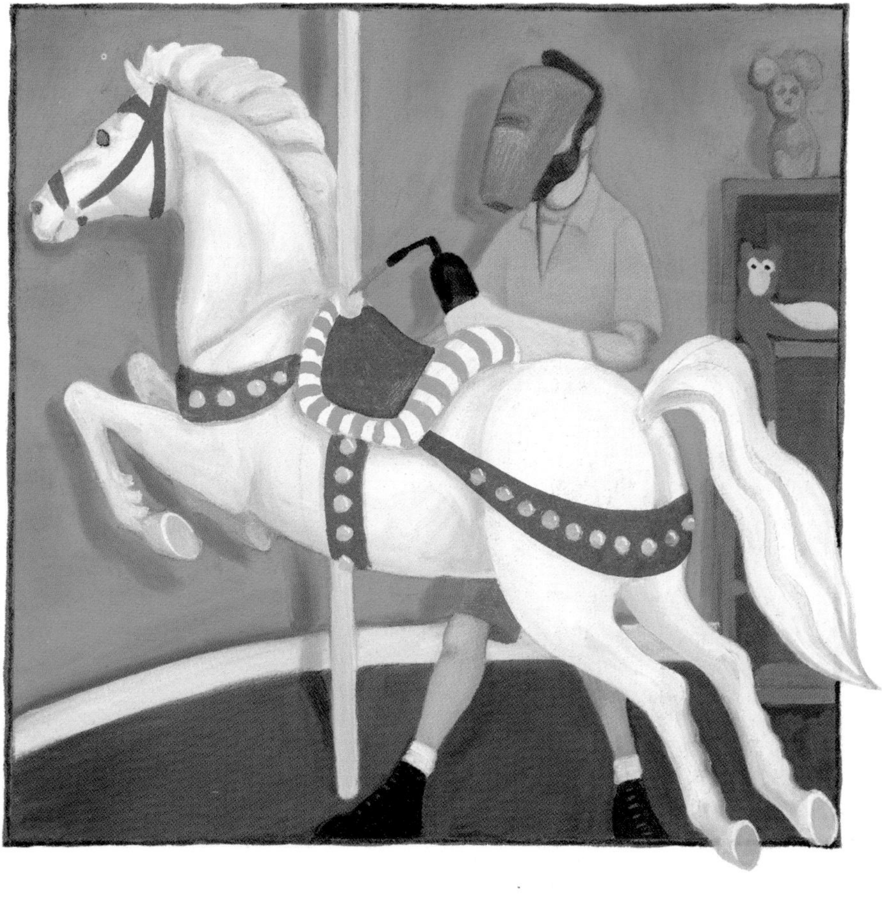

The man made a
merry-go-round.

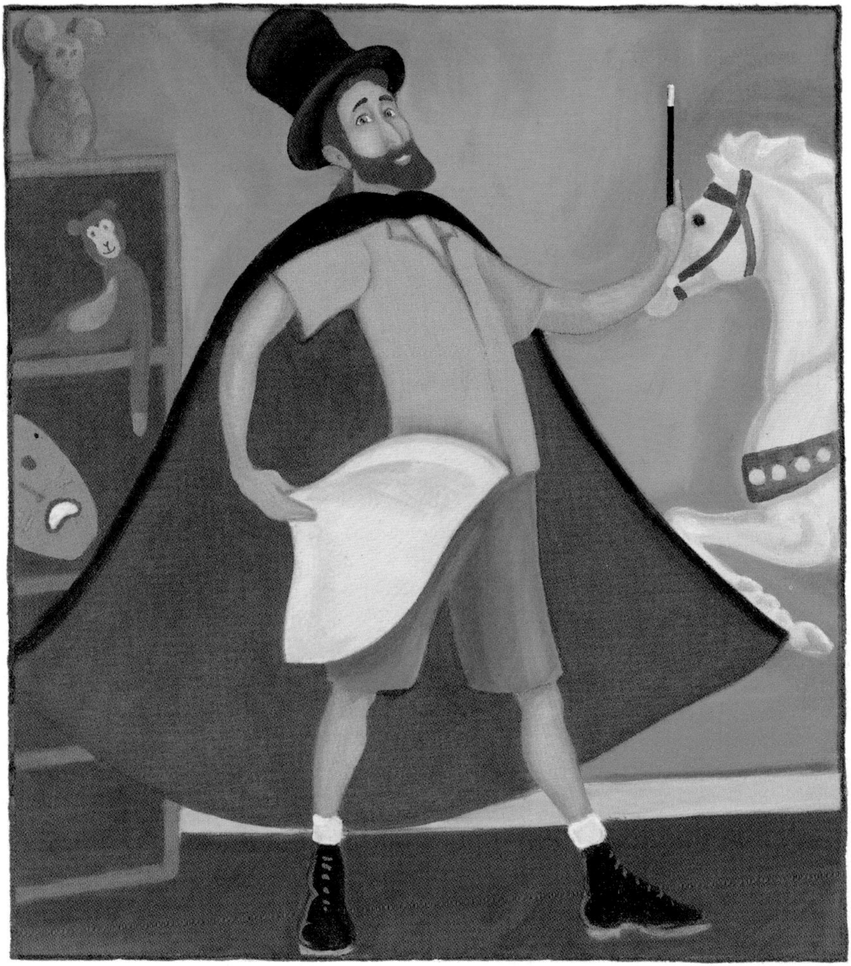

The man made a magic trick.

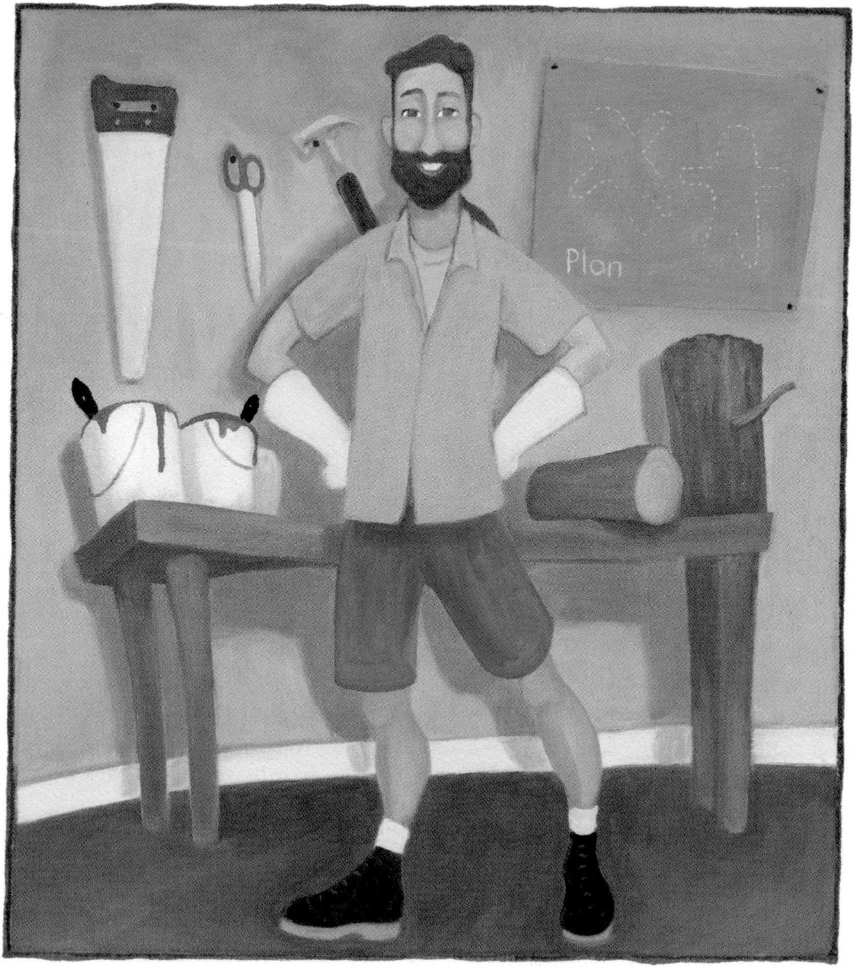

The man made...

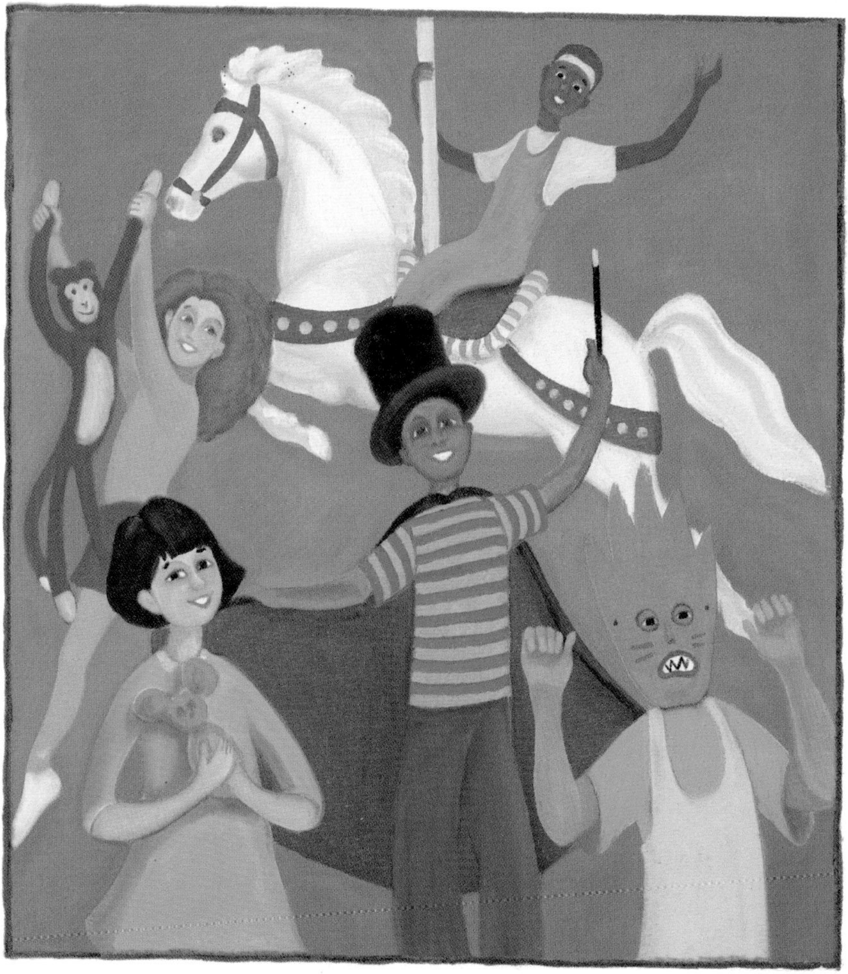

...some friends.